CRUSHING SECRETS

BRADFORD CATHEY

SPEEDY TURTLES PUBLISHING

Copyright © 2024 by Bradford Cathey

All rights reserved.

No portion of this book may be reproduced in any form without written permission from the publisher or author, except as permitted by U.S. copyright law.

Cover photo by Tengyart on Unsplash

Cover design by Bradford Cathey

Acknowledgements

Thank you to my family — for your support, encouragement, and love. I am incredibly blessed and treasure each of you.

Thank you to JG, KB, CB, MM, and KW for reading and proofing the drafts. Your input was crucial to the end product, and I appreciate the gift of your time and energy to me and to this project.

Also...

Thanks be to God, who knows our deepest secrets and yet still loves us completely. While we don't understand why such bad and terrible things happen, we trust that God will hold us close and bring us through.

contents

Introduction	1
THE DRIVE THERE	3
1. On the Road	5
2. Mom	7
3. Dad	9
4. Derek	11
5. Me	13
6. Julia	16
THE VISIT	19
7. Arrival	21
8. Connections	23
9. Heirlooms	26
10. First Strike	29
11. Football and Santa	32
THE DRIVE HOME	35
12. The Dare	37

| 13. Boat Trouble | 40 |
| 14. The D Word | 42 |

THE FIREWORKS — 45

15. Family Traditions	47
16. Firecrackers	50
17. Yelling Through the Door	52
18. The Shot	54

THE MORNING AFTER — 57

19. Waking Up to a Nightmare	59
20. Discovery	61
21. Drop-off	63

THE AFTERMATH — 67

22. Hospital	69
23. No Questions	71
24. Rationale	76
25. Denied	79
26. Aces	84

THE ESCALATION — 87

27. Ramping Up	89
28. Deer Hunt	91
29. Under His Thumb	93
30. Ditch	95

31. Carrying	97
32. Remodel	100
33. Garage	102
THE ESCAPE AND RETURN	105
34. Enlisted	107
35. Legal Woes	109
36. College	112
37. Leaving	114
38. Vegas	117
39. Unbearable Life	119
40. Train Tracks	121
REFLECTIONS	125
41. Dad	127
42. Friendships	131
43. Family Matters	133
Epilogue	135
Afterword	137
Resources	141

Introduction

Elvis Presley once said, "The truth is like the sun. You can shut it out for a time, but it ain't going away."

I have done my dead-level best to shut out the truth for over 40 years. I have denied it, buried it, and run from it. It has chained me, choked me, and crippled me. It has found me high, jailed, and homeless. But like Elvis claimed, the truth just won't go away.

So now, through these pages and for the first time... I am embracing the truth in hopes of finding healing.

THE DRIVE THERE

1
On the Road

We pulled out of the circular driveway in front of our house, and turned right. It was Christmas Eve, 1982. Living in the south, our Christmases weren't characterized by snow and cold temps and sleigh rides. A white Christmas in the Deep South would indeed have been a true Christmas miracle! My town was never short on decorations, however. The brick-covered streets of downtown were adorned with wreaths and lights on each electric pole. Candy canes and bows covered the store windows. Decorations hung suspended over Main Street. Santa participated in our town Christmas parade. Even without the white fluffy stuff, there was no mistaking the season. It was Christmas time.

The trees of the piney woods that characterized our corner of the state became a blur as we picked up speed on the two-lane highway headed southeast. My town was fairly small — only 15,000 people — so it didn't take very long for us to pass by the city limits sign. As we settled in for the 2-hour drive to my grandparents' house, I tried to tune out the adversarial dialogue going on in the front seat between my mom and dad.

My little sister and brother, who were 10 and 8 years old, constantly squirmed beside me in the back seat, relentlessly forcing my attention back inside the car. I had begun counting telephone polls to pass the time, but never got above 23 before being interrupted in one way or another.

My parents arguing wasn't foreign to me. It had been going on for quite some time. Actually pretty much as long as I could remember. The arguments varied in intensity and in the last three or four years, they had escalated to frequent physical contact.

My mom was a school teacher; my dad, a multi-vocational man. They had met at a church revival where my dad was preaching. After dating for a while, she chose to attend the same college where he was studying, and by her senior year they were married.

A few years later, I came along. That was 16 and a half years ago.

2

mom

My mom was a saint.

I never had her as a teacher in the school classroom. But I did have her as a teacher of life. She showed me simple things like how to sign my name in cursive with a little flair. It's a style I still use to this day. Some people have even told me that my handwriting looks like a girls. I'm fine with that, as it reminds me of my mom.

Anything that wasn't macho, she taught me... manners, norms, and proper etiquette. She imparted the importance of respecting people and being polite. She also showed me the importance of neatness. Even now, my environment is generally always neat, concise, and organized. Nothing out of place or erratic. My style is her doing.

I never met any of her former students who had anything bad to say about her. Well, except for one friend who claimed that she got so embarrassed one day that she peed her pants in her classroom. As retrospectively funny as this is, it is the worst thing anyone has ever told me about my mom.

Mom was one of two 1st grade teachers at the school. Some of my favorite memories come from the days just before the school year would start. I would go into the school with her and helping her get her classroom ready – hanging up the alphabet and various educational posters. I would help arrange the desks and label books and organize supplies. I will never forget the smell of freshly laminated posters, chalk dust, and mimeograph copies with purple ink.

She recruited volunteers to come spend time in her classroom as helpers and aides, so that she could spend extra precious minutes with anyone who was having trouble mastering the material or tasks. I can't count the number of times when we would be at the store or somewhere out in public, and one of her students would see my mom and run over to give her a huge hug! The student's parents would always thank my mom for the extra time she had spent with their child in learning something difficult like math or spelling. Mom treated and loved every one of her students like she did her own kids. Many days she would come home exhausted from chasing hyper 1st graders around all day, but she rarely complained.

There were a few of her students over the years that would not have gotten Christmas gifts were it not for my mom. She was keenly aware of the needs of her kids, and would go to great lengths to help meet them. The stack of presents under our own tree might be a little less, but she demonstrated compassion for us and showed us how we should treat others.

She always held these big holiday parties for her students, too. Lots of celebration and happiness could be found in her classroom. There were always leftover cakes, candies, and brownies that she would bring home for us kids. I loved the aftermath of her classroom party days!

3
Dad

If my mom was a saint, then my dad was a devil.

Seriously.

For all the good that my mom did, it came out of the kindness of her heart. For the good that my dad did? It was either self-serving or he did it to convince people to like him or it was with the expectation of a returned favor.

The incredible disconnect was that no one saw this side of my dad except those of us who lived under his roof. To the casual observer, he was a respected community figure. To his congregation, he was a man of God. To fellow business men and women, he was both successful and driven. But to his family? He was a monster.

Dad was abusive, violent, selfish, and chauvinistic. His temper was short and his impatience was ugly. He seemed to think anything he wanted was rightfully his, so he would figure out a way to get it. We saw his sense of this entitlement in his extramarital affairs, in his business dealings, and even in his churches.

I wish that I could tell you I am exaggerating, but I can't. The man who lived in our house was completely different than the man everyone else thought they knew. He was smart, shrewd, and calculating. So much that no one ever thought the wiser. So much so that he was selected as "Man of the Year" for our town by the Chamber of Commerce. So much that people even today, continue to talk fondly about him.

I call B.S.

4
Derek

About 20 minutes into our drive, Derek poked Julia in the ribs for the thousandth time.

"Mom-meeeee!" She squealed.

The car became uncomfortably silent.

"If I have to pull over and stop this car for you kids to be quiet, I will," Dad threatened. Glaring into the back seat through the rear-view mirror, he added "Trust me, you don't want that to happen."

Mom placed her hand on his forearm in an attempt to calm him down a bit. Dad continued driving. Mom looked straight ahead. Julia stuck her tongue out at Derek and grinned. Me? I just rolled my eyes and returned to counting the telephone poles.

Derek was the baby of the family. And also the favorite. Everyone loved "cute little Derek," and of course it was impossible for his 8-year-old self to do anything wrong. In addition to being a good-looking kid, he was athletically talented, already winning races for the local swim club team. He was smart, quick, and resourceful. Basically a very likable kid.

Of course as his older brother, I had responsibilities to fulfill. I would make it a point to play with him, spend time with him, and teach him the ropes. But I would also tease, harass, and bug the daylights out of him. It was my way of keeping him in line.

Since he was so highly favored, I was somewhat surprised that my dad reacted the way he did. He usually just ignored us kids unless he had an agenda.

Mom and Dad were Derek's biological parents; Julia and I had both been adopted as infants. Between that fact, in addition to being the baby, it is understandable why Derek was so coddled and cherished. I know that sounds cliché but it doesn't mean it wasn't true.

5

me

I mentioned that I was adopted. There is actually quite a bit more to that story. Things I had never known until a few months earlier.

On my 16th birthday earlier that year, my mom pulled me into her room and shut the door for privacy.

"I want to tell you something. It's time you know the truth."

I was caught a bit off guard. "Okay."

"Around 17 years ago, your father had a fling with someone. She ended up getting pregnant." Mom continued, "You are their child."

"What?" I responded, "Why are you telling me this?"

Mom continued to explain that around the time I was conceived, my father was quickly becoming a well-known Baptist minister in our region. So it makes sense that getting someone pregnant outside of his marriage would definitely hinder his career, to say the least. When his mistress confronted him with the news, he did what came most natural to him.

He covered it up.

Sadly, my biological mom died just after giving birth to me. But one should never count my dad out. He was somehow able to arrange to make it appear that he and his wife (the person now telling me this) adopted me. Therefore, I was legally adopted by them.

You could have knocked me over with a feather. I was absolutely stunned. Never in my wildest imagination did I suspect he was my biological dad!

I had been born in St. Catherine's Hospital on the 3rd floor. Every time we drove by it, my parents would point out the exact window where I came into the world. I always wondered how they knew the exact room, since I had been adopted; but I never thought to ask. Well, I now no longer had to wonder... Mystery solved.

I took a deep breath, and then exhaled slowly.

"Why are you telling me this now?" I asked her.

"I have had all I can take of your father... his behavior, affairs, and dishonesty. I have been hiding money away, a little at a time. And I finally have saved enough to file for divorce," she stated matter-of-factly. "The papers have been prepared, but nothing has been filed yet. I wanted to tell you the truth myself. I didn't want you finding out from him or be confused by the hate and mudslinging that is sure to happen. I love you as if you were my own blood. I always have, and I always will."

She continued. "When the time comes, the judge may ask you who you want to live with. So I wanted to give you a heads up. Your dad and I will have to negotiate custody of Julia and Derek."

"I want to live with you!" I blurted out. "Please tell me that will happen."

"I can't promise you anything, but I definitely want you with me, too," she responded. "For now, continue to act as if nothing has changed. I just didn't want you to be caught off guard by everything."

6

Julia

My parents voices began to get louder and louder the longer we drove. My mom asking him when he was going to stop cheating on her. Dad throwing back reasons and accusations of his own. Name-calling. Shaming. Blaming. Yelling.

We were about halfway into our drive, when Dad's anger finally peaked. He reached over to grab my mom, and she fended off his arm with her foot. She missed and ended up kicking the gear shift which immediately locked up the tires. I was amazed we didn't wreck!

As we sat there in the back seat on the shoulder of the road, Julia started crying and Derek sat as still as stone. After a few awkward moments, my dad shifted the car back into drive and we started moving again. Derek began to flip through his comic book, knowing he better not make another peep. Julia kept quiet and stared down at her hands in her lap, her lip quivering silently.

I looked over at her hands, too. They were still small, but nothing as tiny as they were when I first saw them.

The day we adopted Julia, I was about six years old. I remember sitting in the hallway on a waiting room couch, while my parents were in the office signing the documents. I looked up from the book I was holding to see the nurses rolling a basket down the hall toward me.

"Do you want to see why your parents are in the office?" the tall, slender nurse asked me in a sing-songy voice.

"Sh-sure?" I responded hesitantly.

Much to my dismay, when I peered over the edge of the bassinet I saw this tiny bundle of a human.

"I thought we were here to get my pupppppppy," I whined. "They promised me a puppy!"

The words that came out of my mouth set off a chain reaction: the nurses began laughing, Julia started crying, and my parents emerged from the office to see what was happening. I was so embarrassed I could have crawled under the couch.

I did get my puppy three days later.

Soon the familiarity of the buildings leading into my grandparents' little town signaled we were almost there. My dad steered our car onto their gravel driveway. We had made it in one piece. Barely. The holiday would now officially begin.

THE VISIT

7

Arrival

As if we had rehearsed our arrival and entrance for months, we all climbed out of the car with smiling faces as if it had been a great drive. My dad turned on his charm and charisma and my mom's mood rose to meet the occasion. Julia ran to hug grandma and Derek high-fived my uncle as he helped him out of the car. I did what most teenagers would do. I stretched and yawned, and rolled my eyes when everyone commented how much I had grown since they had seen me last.

I looked up to see my grandfather coming out the door to join everyone greeting us. He was a cotton and soybean farmer, along with holding the office of the local Justice of the Peace. My grandmother was a farmer's housewife, and they were the parents of six. My mom was the youngest of their children, and her brothers and sisters adored her. They took their responsibility to watch out for her and protect her seriously. Even long after she was "all grown up."

As everyone began filing into the house, I jogged over to the barn and hopped on one of the bikes leaned up against its side. I didn't bother pushing it around to the gravel driveway. Instead I started pedaling furiously across the grass shortcut to reach the road. With a cool breeze in my face, I felt free for a few moments. I was a little more stressed from all of the arguing in the car than I had realized. This momentary escape felt good.

When I was younger, my family had lived in a kid-friendly neighborhood. You know, the kind where you could bike just about anywhere with your buddies as long as you were back home when the streetlights came on. What I would give to be back there again – carefree, lots of friends, and a home that was relatively happy.

That happy home lasted until I was about 11. We had moved into a new house that we built in what was undoubtedly considered the most prestigious neighborhood in town at the time. It was necessary to know the right person, and have that person actually know and like you back, in order to even purchase a lot in that neighborhood.

My dad had all the necessary connections.

8
connections

Growing up, it didn't take me long to realize that my dad was connected to a lot of important and powerful people. He was related to seemingly everyone in our parish, for starters. His position as a juvenile probation officer gave him legal system ties. His work in the tax assessor's office gave him political alliances. And let's not forget, he was a minister. That is a golden ticket in the South.

As a kid, I spent as much time hanging out in the sheriff's office as I probably did going to school. I would shoot the breeze with all the deputies, play card games, and raid the vending machines. They knew me well and I had a lot of fun being around those men. I was "Edward's boy." And I was spoiled by everyone there.

Dad's friendship with a state congressman provided countless trips to the congressman's house, ranch, and office in Baton Rouge. Food, drinks, and sport abounded at all the gatherings and I enjoyed every minute. I loved doing all those things! But I also recognized that my friends didn't have the same experiences I was having.

Dad was related to so many people in our part of the state. Brothers, cousins, uncles were all over the place. And many of them also held positions of influence... law enforcement, religion, and politics.

Over the years, having my friends come over to my house had almost ebbed to a halt. The yelling and arguments between my mom and dad had increased. They were louder and more violent as in throwing objects and breaking things. No longer did they occur only behind closed doors or out of the presence of the kids. I had spent enough time at my friends' houses by then to realize that *my* normal wasn't so normal. I saw my friends' loving families. They had normal arguments, but no fighting or major problems. They were so much different than my own. Different to the point that I longed to stay with them in their homes and not return to my own.

I found myself beginning to make excuses why my friends couldn't come over and I tried my best to keep them away from my house. My home was big and nice and everything. It was the family inside it that embarrassed me and that I was ashamed of. I didn't want anyone else to know how my family acted and what my home was really like. There were way too many secrets that were held there.

By middle school, my dad had begun helping me out in keeping my friends away. The times that I did have a friend or friends over, he would hover around us, simply waiting for a chance to intentionally embarrass me or run off my friends. I'm sure he also wanted to make sure that I wasn't sharing any family secrets, not revealing the problems my family had.

Only a handful of guys ever saw my dad's anger toward me and also the abuse. I saw the shock and surprise in their eyes when that would happen. I usually found a way to brush the incident off or play it off as if it wasn't a big deal. But even my best covers and quick thinking didn't stop them from leaving in a hurry sometimes.

9
Heirlooms

After circling the pond a couple of times, I rode back to the house. I didn't want to be gone too long and create any trouble. I had gotten pretty good at sensing tension and was obsessed with trying to keep the peace in my family.

Although we tried our best to pull off an "everything is fine" charade, I guess the tension between my mom and dad was palpable. My grandpa and grandma asked me more than once that day, "Is everything okay? What is going on?"

It had been hammered into me from early on that you don't let anyone else, even close relatives, in on family matters. My dad's backhand to my face had reinforced that lesson a few times. So instead of being honest about everything with my grandparents, I quelled their inquiries and concern by chalking it up to the fact that my mom didn't really like Christmas-time very much.

She had lost a child — my older sister — on Christmas Day. It wasn't just the anniversary date that caused her sadness, but the whole season. After hearing Christmas music the entire time she was in labor and then giving birth to a stillborn daughter, who could blame her? Everything Christmas brought her flashbacks and grief. However, even in the midst of her own pain, she somehow found ways to help us understand and experience the true joy of Christmas.

So when I referred to my mom's pain as the reason for things being off, my responses to their concerns were completely believable.

I walked toward the back of the house through the kitchen. It was filled with delicious smells — the glazed ham baking in the oven, the apples pies cooling on the counter, and the sugary marshmallows on top of the sweet potato casserole.

Mom wasn't where I thought I would find her out on the back porch, so I started looking for her around the house. I finally found mom upstairs in the attic. She was gathering some of her childhood things and packing them in boxes... things like an old toy wagon, a doll collection, and other favorite belongings from when she was young. When I asked her what she was doing, she told me that she was taking them home. She wanted to make sure that Julia received them as heirlooms.

As I left to head back downstairs, I overheard her talking to her sister. I stopped on the third or fourth step and remained still.

"Edward and I are finished. I just can't live with the way my marriage is anymore." Mom continued, "he's never going to stop the affairs. And I'm afraid one of these times when he hits me, I might not wake up."

After a long pause and what I could only assume was her sister comforting her with a quiet hug, she instructed my aunt. "If anything bad happens to me, get Evan out of the house and away from Edward. And tell him to find and bring my diaries to you."

There were many of them. Mom would write in her journal every day and she would keep them in her end table. Then at the end of the year, she would take all those journals and put them in a shoe box, write the year on the shoebox and store them in the closet on the top shelf. Each January 1st would start off with a fresh journal and a new year.

My mom was clever. She had a habit of writing in her diary almost daily. But she didn't trust my dad to keep from meddling with things that were extremely private to her. To make her diary seem mundane, she had enmeshed the crummy stories and happenings — things that would incriminate my dad — in between her normal journal entries.

As I stood silently on the stairs, I realized. Mom was letting Aunt Martha know how to find out the truth about our lives.

10
First Strike

The first time I saw my dad slap my mom, I was 13. I had always been big for my age and was a strong as ox, so I ran in and separated them and stood in the middle to protect mom. The result? Two black eyes for me and a broken nose for Dad. But he sure as heck didn't slap her again that night.

I became her self-appointed protector from that moment on. At least to the extent that it was possible. I was now big enough to fend off dad. Or at the very least I could inflict some damage back onto him.

Unfortunately, what I didn't understand at that moment was that I placed myself in his sights as the primary target of his anger.

Once our yard got rolled — that is, toilet paper thrown into the trees — in an epic fashion by a bunch of my friends. I believe the rumor was that they used 96 rolls! Impressive to say the least.

When we woke up that morning, my dad was livid. He ordered me to go clean it up. He said it made our yard look trashy. I must not have done a good enough job in his opinion cleaning up the first time, so he beat me with a belt. My second clean-up attempt was not fast enough for him, so he hit me with a baseball bat.

Mom could do nothing to help me, but only plead and beg him to stop.

Not too long after that, he bashed my knee with a piece of firewood. I honestly can't remember why. But I do know that I was in a full leg cast for several months. The explanation to those outside the family when asked, was that my cast was due to a "football injury."

The code of silence around Dad's abuse was understood. Neither my brother nor sister ever spoke of it. My mom couldn't say anything either. One of the realities of living with an abuser is that asking for help often only makes the abuse worse. I think that's why so many people stay in relationships that hurt them. Fear of greater harm than they are already experiencing.

The day that I brought home my first-ever "B" on a report card, I got punched in the head and called names until I passed out.

"Dumbass."

"Stupid."

"Failure."

I was frequently reminded after that beating, that our family "didn't make B's." So out of spite... yep. The next term I made an F on purpose. But boy did I pay for it. Dad beat me with a rope and his fist, on and off for two days. Of course the school believed the reason for my 4-day absence was because I had "the flu."

I have had ribs busted, my nose broken, two broken arms, a smashed knee, and way too many other cuts, bumps, and bruises to list. All thanks to my dear old Dad.

My dad - A pillar of our community. An elected official. A minister of God. But what I saw and experienced was that he was a piece of shit. The devil on earth. My #1 enemy.

It was extremely difficult to hear other people often admire, praise, and applaud my dad. To watch him be given awards and public respect. It made me resent those people and even kind of hate them for embracing and elevating my dad to sainthood.

If they only really knew him.

11
Football and Santa

Derek ran into the parlor where I was lying in front of the television with the football. "Can we play, Evan? Pleeeeease?" he whined.

"Sure," I told him, picking him up from behind and pretending to body slam him onto the couch.

"Not tackle!" He giggled.

I chased him out into the back yard. Most everyone filed outside after us and joined in, either playing or cheering or laughing.

After a fun game of touch football in my grams' back yard, we all headed back inside for dessert. The sun was setting and we would need to hit the road soon.

While we were gathered around the table, Julia inquired. "Do you think Santa has left the North Pole yet?" Then Derek chimed in. "How long does it take him to make it all around the world?"

"All I know," pronounced my grandfather in his slow deliberate manner, "is that if you are not asleep when he gets to your house, his reindeer will fly him away. No matter how many reindeer carrots and Santa cookies you may leave out."

"Mommy, we need to leave SOON!" Julia begged. "I really really want Santa to bring me a Barbie Bubble Bath and Dream House!"

"And I asked him for a Hulk Hogan action figure and a guitar," Derek chimed in.

"Evan, what do you want for Christmas?" My grandmother asked me.

I thought about saying what I really wanted aloud. But I knew that speaking of my dad's behavior would only make things worse. So I paused for a moment and then responded softly, "I'd love to have a Sony Walkman."

"Time to go," my dad interrupted. It was as if he read what I was thinking and decided to eliminate the risk of my spilling the beans. He was always on top of controlling the situation.

We hugged everyone goodbye, said our "I love you's and Merry Christmases" and climbed into the car.

"Merry Christmas!!" Derek called once more, leaning halfway out of the car. "And Happy New Year!!"

THE DRIVE HOME

12

The Dare

We were all smiling and waving as we pulled out of the driveway. But as soon as our car was out of sight from my grandparents house, the arguing between my parents returned with a fury.

"What is all that crap that you loaded in the trunk?" My dad started in. "You don't need to bring more clutter into our house. There's enough junk there already."

My mom replied nonchalantly, "It's just some things I decided to bring home for Julia. They have nothing to do with you."

My dad muttered something under his breath, but none of us could hear what he said. I looked over at him from my seat. I was riding shotgun now, and mom was in the back seat with my brother and sister. His eyes narrowed as he flipped on the headlights and turned onto the highway that would lead us home.

The sun dropped just below the horizon, and I settled in for the long ride ahead and leaned my head against the window.

The last road trip I had been on was back in the summer. My church youth choir had taken a trip to Washington, D.C. We travelled in style in a chartered coach bus, stopping along the way to sing and stay in homes of local families.

Once we made it to the D.C., our director had us scheduled to play handbells in the Rotunda of the Senate Building, sing on the steps of the Capitol, and other musical events. We also toured some of the monuments together.

Amazingly enough, we were also allowed some free time to explore on our own as long as we stayed in groups of three or more. For the most part, we stayed within the parameters we were given. But what teenager could resist a side trip via the Metro to the Pentagon?

One day, while some of us were walking away from the Lincoln Memorial, a couple of my buddies ran ahead of me and stopped me in my tracks.

"We double dog dare you to jump into in the Reflection Pool!"

And then, noticing my initial hesitation they added, "Twenty bucks for you if you'll do it."

I paused. I didn't really need the money. But I had placed a long-distance phone call to my mom just hours before, and I could tell from the sound of her voice that she had been crying. I knew this was most likely the result of an argument with my dad that had turned physical. Maybe, just maybe, I thought to myself, pulling a shenanigan such as this would get me sent home by our director? Then I could be back at home to protect my mom from my dad.

So, I went for it. I slowly took off my shoes and then my socks and stepped in. I began to wade a few feet out from the edge. Friends laughed, cameras snapped, and strangers took notice. Then I slowly sat down and leaned back into the water. I came up from below the water to applause and cheering and more laughter. I exhaled out a long slow breath. This would definitely piss off Mr. Eddy enough to send me home as a consequences for my bad choice. And I wouldn't have to say a word for him to find out. I was drenched from head to toe.

About 10 minutes later, as my luck would have it, the skies opened up and rain poured down. By the time we got back to our hotel to meet up with the chaperones, everyone was as completely soaked as I was. Oh well. My best laid plans for an early departure.

13

Boat Trouble

That same summer, we had taken Dad's ski boat to the lake. The plan was for him to come out later and bring Derek and Julia. He asked my friends and me to go early and get out on the lake to beat the crowd. The park placed a limit on how many boats could be launched at any given time.

My friends and I had big plans for the day. Skiing. Swimming. Goofing off. A fun day on the lake. But that never happened.

Just after getting the boat in the water and making one quick ski run, the prop on the boat fell off. Dad had changed it out during the week. But he had failed to put the cotter pin back through the shaft in order to hold the nut securely. But that didn't matter. When he arrived, he blamed me for it and blew up in a tirade. My friends saw his behavior and quickly decided it was time to call it a day and head home.

Dad, Derek, and Julia left soon too, leaving me alone with the boat, the trailer, and the truck.

I had to swim with the tow rope and bring the boat back to the launch ramp, muscle the boat onto the trailer, then drive the truck home. When I arrived home, Dad beat me so bad I ended up having to miss youth camp that year. No one needed to see my black eye and fractured arm. It would only solicit questions. Questions that I had no interest in trying to deflect.

Back in the car, as the Christmas Eve stars began to appear out my window, I looked up at the sky. I rubbed my hand over the small bump on my arm where it had healed from last summer, remembering Dad's anger. I looked over at my dad behind the wheel, shook my head, and gazed back up at the stars.

"I wish I may, I wish I might... have a normal family tonight."

14

The D Word

Just as we pulled into the driveway of our house, Mom broke the silence.

"Edward. I want a divorce."

My guess is that she waited until we were home because she didn't know what Dad might do if he were still driving.

He blew up, of course.

Actually, I should really say that he exploded. His eyes grew red and the veins in his neck bulged out. He immediately started yelling and swearing and slamming his hand on the steering wheel.

Thankfully mom was in the backseat with Derek and Julia on the way home, and out of his immediate reach on the opposite side of the car.

As Dad turned around to confront her, she quickly bolted from the car. As soon her door opened, I quickly hit the power lock button locking the rest of the doors. It didn't make much of a difference, but it did give her a few second head start ahead of

Dad to get to the safety of their bedroom. That's all she needed. Once there, she slammed and locked the door.

We all sat in stunned silence for a minute, then piled out of the car and walked inside. We followed Dad through the house to her door. He could have easily kicked it in, as it was merely a typical knob lock. But he refrained from doing so – at least not in front of Derek and Julia.

He slammed me against the wall with his forearm as he turned to walk away from the bedroom door. Then my dad retreated into his man cave and bolted that door shut.

So. There we were on Christmas Eve. Mom locked in the master bedroom on one end of the house and Dad locked in his man cave on the other end. The three of us kids were left just standing in the middle, looking blankly at one another while the multi-colored lights of our tree reflected in our eyes.

I realized then we needed a miracle. Something even Santa couldn't provide.

THE FIREWORKS

15

Family Traditions

The traditional family happenings on Christmas Eve and Christmas morning in our house went like this. As soon as the littles were fast asleep, my dad and I would play Santa and the elf. We would retrieve the Santa purchases from our hiding places around the house, assemble anything that needed to be assembled and place batteries in the things that required them. Once we had set out all the toys and gifts where they belonged, I would return to my room while Dad put my things out. We all recognized that in order to keep Julia and Derek believing, Santa had to pay big brother a visit, too!

On Christmas morning, we would all make breakfast and deliver breakfast-in-bed to my mom. While in my parents' room, we would listen to the reading of the *real* Christmas story. Following that, we would go down the hall as a family to enter the living room where the tree and presents and Santa gifts were waiting. Dad would film the excitement with the latest video camera available, as the blanket was pulled aside from the opening to the room and Derek and Julia would run in to check out their toys.

Christmas Eve night was no different in regards to Santa than it had been in years past. The kids fell asleep relatively fast. Even though the excitement of Santa was definitely coursing through their minds, the day had been full of activity and play for them. They were tired.

Dad eventually emerged from his man cave and he and I placed all of Santa's goodies for the kids around the tree. We worked in silence, as I was extremely careful to not say anything that might set him off again.

Not long after we finished setting up Santa, I was hanging out in my room playing Pole Position on my Atari. My room was on the same end of the house as our garage, and just across the hall from dad's man cave. Suddenly, the squelch of the police scanner stationed in his cave broke my concentration.

"Dispatch to WS-6."

"WS-6, copy."

"Be advised that two inmates escaped 10 minutes ago. They are both white males. One 5'10" with brown hair, brown eyes. The other is 6'2" with black hair and mustache. Witnesses claim to have seen both individuals heading west out of town on Hwy 28."

"10-4. I'll head that direction now."

My dad was silent. So I entered his room to find him seated in his big recliner.

"Did they just say what I thought they said?" I asked excitedly.

"Yeah, apparently two guys are on the loose, and..." The ringing of our telephone interrupted my dad.

The one-sided conversation didn't enlighten me much at all about the situation, but I had not doubt who was on the other end of the line: someone at the sheriff's office.

"Yes."

"What time?"

"Anything I can do?"

"Okay, keep me posted."

I waited for my dad to tell me more, but after he hung up the phone, he just leaned back into the cushions of his recliner and stared up at the ceiling fan. I took that as an indication for me to leave, and went back into my room, unpaused my game and continued to play.

The time was 10:48pm.

16

Firecrackers

Derek and Julia were cuddled up in their sleeping bags in the family den, rather than their own rooms. It was Christmas Eve, so the special privilege of "camping out" on the floor was a fun event.

About 11:15, I was startled to hear firecrackers popping outside of our house. I should mention that most of the people our little town LOVED our fireworks! In the early 80's, there were no huge corporate-run firework shows for July 4th, Christmas, and New Years in small towns like there are these days. But we never had any trouble creating our own entertainment. From bottle rockets to black cats and blooming flowers to Roman candles. It's actually amazing that we survived those experiences with our fingers and eyes intact. One of our favorite tricks was to light a whole pack of firecrackers - 30, 75, 250, the bigger the better - and drop them on someone's front porch. Then run like hell. Nothing but rapid fire pops and flashes, the smell of gunpowder, and a whole lot of laughing among friends.

That's what I was hearing now... a small pack of Black Cats exploding right outside our door. On any other night I wouldn't have thought twice about the possibility that some of my friends were pranking me. But it was Christmas Eve. All of my friends would be at home with their families, not out together causing trouble. And definitely not that late on Christmas Eve.

A little while later, more firecrackers started popping outside my bedroom window. My first thought, "Oh great. I'm definitely gonna get blamed for this shit."

But surprisingly Dad just stuck his head in my door a few moments later. I watched through slitted eyes, acting as if I were asleep and praying silently that he would just leave.

Thankfully, he did.

17
Yelling Through the Door

Minutes later, I could hear him yelling at my mom through their bedroom door. I eased my way into the family room to be within better earshot.

"You cannot divorce me!!"

"Do you understand what that will do to me politically? Vocationally?"

"You can count on going back to being the poor-ass daughter of a dirt farmer. You'll see!"

"Just stop this foolishness! I'm the best thing that ever happened to you!"

I never heard my mom. Maybe she was responding but I just couldn't hear her.

A few minutes later, he returned to the door and continued. He claimed his affairs had been meaningless. He pledged his love for my mom. He threatened, begged, and swore to God in Heaven.

Finally, it was silent. I suddenly realized he was heading back to our end of the house. So I ran back to my room, jumped into bed under the covers, and faked being asleep once again. Amazingly, Derek and Julia slept soundly. Through all of the commotion.

I heard the garage door opening. Eight seconds of rumbling and squeaking. Then, another round of fireworks. "Pow! Pow! Pow! Pow! Pow!" in rapid succession. I heard the garage door close back down as the last few popped.

For a third time, Dad stuck his head in my door. He saw me "sleeping" and eased back out, but left my door ajar this time.

Even with my door only slightly open, I had a direct clear view from my bed out into the family room. I could also see through to the door that led to the utility room. The utility room door was open as well, and the dining room light was on, providing plenty of enough light for me to see clearly.

18

THE SHOT

I did a double-take and sat up quickly when I saw Dad pass through the kitchen walking toward mom's end of the house. In his hand was a shotgun.

My mom hated guns. She never even touched so much as a toy cap gun. We were never allowed to play with toy guns as kids. Heck, I was 15 before she finally allowed me to have a hunting gun. All of my friends had gotten them as younger kids – a rite of passage. My mom certainly didn't know how to load one. And she definitely didn't need one now.

So what the hell was going on?

My heart-rate quickened and I sprang out of my bed. I made sure he didn't see me, then tip-toed quietly behind my dad at a distance.

I jumped when I heard a smash. It must have been the door getting busted open.

Immediately, I heard a screech from Mom.

Then just as I reached the beginning of the hallway and peered around the corner, I saw a FLASH and heard a LOUD BOOM.

I ran back toward my room scared shitless and screaming silently in my head.

Dad must have caught a glimpse of me just as he exited the room into the hallway, and yelled after me.

"Evan!"

I froze in my tracks. Then turned slowly around to face him.

"What are you doing?" I cried. "What was that noise I heard?"

I glanced down at his hands and noticed that he no longer was holding the gun.

"Aw, it must have been fireworks." He replied. "Your damn friends have been popping them all night long. Now get your ass back in bed!"

It was just before midnight.

I hurried toward my bedroom with my dad continuing to follow me. Once I saw my dad turn to go into his man cave, I shut my bedroom door. Not for the first time, I really wished there was a deadbolt lock on it. I was shaking. My heart was racing. I was sweaty and cold at the same time. My throat was dry and scratchy, but there was absolutely no way I was leaving the security of my bedroom to get a glass of water. My head was pounding. If Dad had just shot my mom, I was worried I might be next.

I sat silently on the carpeted floor next to my door and listened closely to hear any movement or activity in the kitchen or den. My head was spinning. I stared at the phone on my bedside table, longing to call someone but knowing everyone would already be asleep. I thought about calling the police, but then reminded myself that I knew better. Someone would surely tip off my dad that I called, then my chances of being alive when they arrived would be less than zero. I grabbed my football and slammed it into my pillow. I screamed silently into the other pillow next to it. Finally crawling under the covers to the foot of my bed, I simply tried to escape into the darkness.

What the hell had just happened? Was my mom going to be okay?

THE MORNING AFTER

19
Waking Up to a Nightmare

Suddenly, Derek came bursting through my door. "It's Christmas morning, Evan!" He shrieked, jumping up on my bed. My brain was foggy. My head hurt and my eyes burned. I didn't think I had actually fallen asleep. I shook my head like a pup trying to dry off. I was trying to shake the cobwebs loose from my mind.

"Who...?"

"What day...?"

"Where...?"

Then it hit me.

Derek dragged me out of bed by my hand and led me into the kitchen where he and Julia had begun making breakfast for mom. It would be toast and jelly and pancakes, with orange juice and coffee. The blanket hung across the formal living room blocking their view of the presents that Santa had delivered.

While my brother and sister were cooking, my dad shouted into the kitchen from his man cave. "Hey Evan! Go make sure Mom is awake."

WHAT???

WAIT.

WHAT???

I squinted my eyes a bit, trying to think clearly of what I should say and do. Was I dreaming? "Wake. Her. Up." What exactly had I seen and heard last night?

As I stood there shifting my weight from one foot to the other, he came into the kitchen and gave me a hard stern look. Through his clinched teeth, he ordered, "Do it." Then grabbing my shoulder firmly, he followed up, "Now."

I walked slowly and deliberately through the living room and foyer and into the hallway. Past the bathroom, Derek's room, the linen closet, and Julia's room. I slowed my steps as I approached the master bedroom. I could see that the door was open just about an inch. I knocked on it softly and it opened more.

20

Discovery

The first thing to hit me was the smell of wet rust and copper. It turned my stomach. It was the same smell I had experienced when wild game was being field dressed after a hunt.

Blood. And guts.

Then I saw her lying on the bed and I couldn't stop myself. I wretched and threw up violently. Forcing my eyes down to avoid seeing my mom's body again, I quickly shut the door, and sprinted back to the kitchen.

Breathless, I looked past my dad to the counter where the pancakes were on the griddle. Julia had just finished flipping the first pancakes, and turned toward me with a proud grin on her face. I wiped my face with my sleeve and hurriedly picked up Derek in my arms. I grabbed Julia's arm with my other hand. "C'mon. Let's go wish Mr. Ronnie and Mrs. Carla a Merry Christmas!"

"But I want to finish cooking and go hear Momma read the Christmas story!" Julia exclaimed, pulling me back toward the kitchen with all of her slight build. "That's what we always do!"

"What about Santa and the presents?" Derek cried, thrashing about on my hip. "I don't want go anywhere! I don't want to leeeeeave!"

I reached to get my keys and Dad grabbed my arm. Hard. As his fingers dug into my tricep, he whisper-growled, "Forget what you may or may not have seen and heard, or you will find yourself being next."

I shook my arm loose from his grip and herded my brother and sister out through the garage, practically shoving them into the cab of my truck. I ran around to the driver's side. My hands were shaking so uncontrollably, it took three tries to get the key into the ignition. Finally, the engine roared to life and rocks flew out from underneath the wheels as I stomped the accelerator down hard and fast. I couldn't get us out of there soon enough.

What the hell was I going to do?

21
Drop-Off

Ronnie and Carla Meyers were probably our closest family friends. They socialized a lot with my parents, and they also had kids around the same ages as us. Thoughts were swirling around my mind... Questions I knew we would face. "Why were we showing up there on Christmas morning? Why weren't my mom and dad with us? Why was I so shaken and sweaty? How was our Christmas morning?" I was incredibly lost. And scared.

When we got to the Meyer's driveway, I haphazardly parked my truck. I helped Derek and Julia out of the cab, and hurriedly walked them to the front door.

I guess Ms. Carla had seen us pull in the driveway, because she opened the door before I even had a chance to ring the doorbell.

Julia was still teary and Derek was continuing to whine about not being able to open presents yet. My face lacked all color and even though I was constantly wiping my palms on my pants leg, they were still sweaty.

"Why, Merry Christmas Kiddos!" she exclaimed. "What in the world are you doing here?" And then quickly, "Come on inside. Come on, come on in!"

Mr. Ronnie stood up from his place on the couch, where he had been installing batteries in a new toy that Tony had received from Santa. "What brings you guys over? Did Santa not come visit you?"

Thankfully, Tony and Sarah's presents and toys had caught the attention of Julia. She ran over and plopped down on the floor. Derek followed. That left me looking ragged, teary-eyed, and completely speechless, simply standing in the foyer with my hands in my pockets.

I slowly walked over to the couch where Mr. Ronnie had been sitting, and took a seat. Quizzical looks from Mr. Ronnie and Ms. Carla continued to meet my eyes. I couldn't tell them what had happened. Hell, I was still trying to figure out and digest everything myself.

So I said the only words that I could muster, "Dad," as I wiped my nose, "will tell you later."

We sat silently, watching the kids all playing and having fun together. It was probably only about 45 minutes, but it seemed like a lifetime. Once or twice, Ms. Carla went into the kitchen to refill their coffee cups. She brought pastries out and offered them to us. I couldn't eat. I couldn't speak. I wasn't even sure that I could continue breathing for much longer. My chest felt like there was an elephant sitting on it.

We heard a car pull into the driveway. Julia ran to look out the front door. "It's Daddy! And Dr. Baker is with him?"

Dr. Baker was the pastor of our church. He was viewed as the entire community's pastor, as he loved everyone and was instrumental in bridging the racial divide that was present in our community. He and the pastor of the black church in town would sometime swap pulpits in a show of unity. He was a really cool and admirable man.

I quickly deduced that one, if my dad was here, the police hadn't arrested him; and two, he must have sold his story to them and to my pastor. I couldn't handle anymore.

As they entered through the front door, I pushed past my dad, hitting his shoulder with mine for emphasis. My eyes met Dr. Baker's but I quickly looked down. I couldn't offer even so much as a "hello" from my lips. I jogged toward my truck and hopped in the cab.

My hands were still shaking. I could barely breathe.

THE AFTERMATH

22

HOSPITAL

I woke up two days later in a hospital bed in another state. I had no idea how I got there except that they told me that I had been in an accident in my truck, and someone had found me unconscious.

"What is your name, son?" The doctor with a thin face and receding hairline asked as he rushed into the room.

I told him my name. The he asked how old I was and where I lived. Thankfully I remembered who I was, as there was no identification on me when they found me. In my rush to leave my house Christmas morning, I had forgotten my wallet.

Lying face up on those crisp white hospital bedsheets, I stared at the ceiling. I slowly started putting the pieces back together in my mind. Christmas Eve day at Grandpa and Grandma's house. Mom and Dad arguing on the way home. Seeing dad taking the gun and entering their bedroom where my mom was. Seeing the flash. Hearing the shot. Discovering Mom. Getting threatened by my dad. Dropping my brother and sister off at a friends' house.

"Shit!" I thought. "What day is this? And where am I?"

I went down a mental checklist in my head:

- My mom is dead.
- My dad killed her.
- He's walking free.
- I'm the only one who knows what really happened.
- Dad will kill my brother and sister if I tell anyone the truth.

"I am up shit creek, and no paddle anywhere in sight," I sighed.

23

NO QUESTIONS

Once I was driven back home, I found out from my friend what had happened after I raced from the house with Derek and Julia on Christmas morning. Police officers had arrived on scene not too long after we left.

Although our house was inside of the city limits, Dad had also called the sheriff's office to report mom's death. He had no influence over the police department, but he had the sheriff's office in his back pocket. Soon, they arrived, too.

Once the sheriff's deputies came into our house, they told the police officers that they were taking over the investigation. They thanked the police for showing up, but sternly told them they were no longer needed.

This little turf war only lasted a couple of minutes, since the sheriff ultimately was the higher authority. The police left quietly, shaking their heads and muttering.

Dad led the sheriff deputies to the bedroom where my mom's body was lying on the bed. He told them that she must have killed herself during the night. He said she had locked the door when they had gotten home that night, as she wasn't feeling well. He claimed he had forced it open when she wouldn't answer his knocking that morning.

The officers looked around, summoned for the coroner, and expressed their condolences to my father. A few moments later, our pastor had arrived. That explained why he was with my dad when they showed up at the Meyers.

***

There was never any real investigation conducted. Hell, there was not even a charade of an investigation! Anyone with half a brain would have questions about what had happened in my home that night.

> Why use a shotgun instead of a handgun? Even then, very few women commit suicide with a firearm.

> Why was the blood splatter in such a location as it was?

> Whose fingerprints were on the gun?

> Why hadn't anyone in the family heard the shot?

What was the current relationship like between my mom and dad?

Did any of the kids see or hear anything unusual?

Were there journals or writings anywhere that would convey her state of mind?

But no one asked questions. Not. A. Single. One.

Maybe it was because they actually believed his story, or at least they wanted to believe it. Maybe it was because the attention of law enforcement was focused on the manhunt for the escaped prisoners who had also just murdered a local couple, and there just wasn't enough manpower to cover another investigation that morning. Maybe it was because they knew my dad held a lot of power over a lot of people, and their status and success depended on keeping my dad happy.

Or. Maybe it was a combination of all of the above and my dad was clever enough to exploit the situation. After all, timing is everything, right?

Regardless, the story everyone subscribed to – whether they were willing participants or simply oblivious to the truth – was that my mom committed suicide.

Newspaper Articles from December 1982

That was the story that everyone knew and accepted: A well-respected community man loses his wife to unexpected suicide on Christmas Eve.

The outpouring from our church family and friends was over the top. It was obvious that my mom had been well-respected and deeply loved. There was more food brought to our house than could feed an army. Countless cards and letters expressing sympathy arrived daily. Flowers were sent to both the funeral home and to our house. Our family room became like a greenhouse.

It all made me sick inside. I knew they wanted us to realize they cared, but the whole thing was all such a cluster. Little did any of them know that their gifts of comfort were being delivered to a murderer.

24
Rationale

Join me in a thought experiment.

Here are the things that would have had to happen in order for my mom to kill herself. My mom — the lady who hated guns and refused to ever touch one — would choose this means to end her own life?

She would have had to...

1. Gain possession of a key to the gun safe. Dad was the only person who had one.

2. Gain possession of key to the ammunition box. Again, would have to obtain from Dad.

3. Figure out which ammo belonged to the gun she chose, and take that.

4. Do all of this without being seen by any of us.

5. Figure out how to load the gun with the shotgun shells.

6. Figure out how to take the safety off and cock the gun.

7. Hold the gun up to her head with the butt, or heavy end, away from her body. Do this with one hand. Nearly impossible for the strongest of individuals. (The blood spatter on the wall indicated she wasn't sitting on the edge of the bed and using her feet to hold it.)

8. Give the keys back to Dad — without tracking any blood through the house.

9. Return to her room, lie down on the far side of the bed, and die.

She didn't do it. It's not rocket science.

25

Denied

I don't really remember much about the rest of the holidays following Mom's funeral. They say that sometimes not remembering things is the way that our brain protects us from the feelings we can't handle.

I do remember going back to school after the New Year. I tried to lay low and not draw any attention to myself. I didn't participate in class discussions as much as I typically would. I made it a point to eat lunch by myself away from my friends. I stayed outside the building until the last possible chance before going inside to class.

But still it felt like everyone was looking at me with pity, as if to say, "that's the kid whose mom killed herself." My face would burn when I felt their eyes focusing in on me. I would break out in a sweat. But I never looked back at them. If my eyes were to meet theirs, I wasn't sure how I would react.

"She didn't kill herself, dammit!"

"Don't feel sorry for me because my mom is gone. Just help me get away from my dad!"

Or worse, I might just burst into tears and run into the bathroom.

So, rather than risk all of those possible scenarios, I withdrew into my own world and blocked out everyone and everything possible.

That served me well for a few days at least until the looks and whispers faded a bit.

***

That same first week in January, things were happening behind the scenes with my mom's side of the family.

My mom's sisters came to town. They went to the Sheriff's department to request a further investigation into the death of my mom.

"Hi, I'm Martha Thomas. Katherine Woods is, I mean *was*, my sister," she introduced herself to the front desk clerk. "And this is our other sister, Louise. We would like to discuss Katherine's case with someone."

Aunt Martha and Aunt Louise were invited to take a seat and wait. A few minutes later, a deputy came out, introduced himself, and invited them back to a small room. There was only a table and four chairs, and the walls were bare.

"Katherine's death does not make sense to us," she began. "We spent all of Christmas Eve day with her. She was not suicidal in any way. We can't believe that she killed herself."

The deputy spoke up, "Well, her death was ruled a suicide. Sometimes people are very good at hiding what is really going on inside and how they are really feeling."

"Maybe so, but I know that Katherine would never ever leave her children. No matter what she may have been feeling. It's just not like her," Aunt Louise responded. "Plus, she *hated* guns. Even if she was suicidal, which I'll never believe she was, she definitely wouldn't have used a gun to do it."

"Were you there at the scene?" Aunt Martha inquired of the deputy.

"No, but I have the report right here," he said, glancing down on the table.

"Well the report is wrong. How do we go about getting ya'll to investigate further?"

The detective leaned back in his chair. "There is nothing to investigate. The case is closed."

***

Martha and Louise then went across the street to the police department. They explained their interactions with the sheriff's department and inquired if there might be anything that the police could do to further investigate the case.

The chief came out and met them. He explained that his hands were tied, that the jurisdiction and investigation belonged to the sheriff's department. He could only provide input if requested by the sheriff.

So they returned to the sheriff's office, and begged that someone at least talk to me about what happened that night, that maybe I might know something that law enforcement was not yet aware of.

"Katherine told me on Christmas Eve afternoon that if anything happened to her, I was to get Evan and to tell him to bring her diaries," Aunt Martha pleaded. "Just talk to him. He *has* to know something."

They were denied again. They were told that unless new evidence was presented, the case would remain closed.

The second denial wasn't surprising, as law enforcement could only talk to a minor with a parent's permission. And they knew my father was definitely not going to let that happen.

My aunts were told that my mom's death was an "open and shut" investigation, and the conclusion was that my mom had committed suicide. The deputy explained he would no longer entertain any more discussion of the matter, and instructed them to leave.

***

But here's the thing. You know how cops are when they want to find out something or when they want to just be inquisitive. They find ways to go around loopholes and accomplish the things that they want to get done, because of a hunch or the feeling something strange is going on.

In the small town community I was in, I knew all the cops. I knew all the deputies. I'd run through all levels of the courthouse.

I'd gone into their houses to party with them, to play with their little kids. I'd grown up with them. Had they wanted to get to me, it wouldn't have been that hard to do. But no one ever did. Back in that day there were lines drawn in the sand. You either chose not to cross them, or if you did cross them, you suffered the consequences.

Nobody crossed the line Dad had drawn around me.

It's also why Dad made sure to tell me and remind me often that he would hurt my friends, my relatives, my brother, my sister. and anybody else around me if the truth got out. Because he knew all it would take for his secret to crumble would be for a respected person in the community to ask me about what happened that night.

26

Aces
Aces

Soon I realized that nothing was going to be done to change the narrative of what happened to my mom or to reveal the truth. This was a situation I was going to have to figure out how navigate if I wanted to stay alive. It was also imperative I played along in order to protect Derek and Julia.

I began to gather some things from around my house. Some things that were sentimental and others that may come in handy were the truth ever to come out.

- 10 family photo albums

- 32 trophies from participation in music, 4-H, FFA, football and such

- mom's senior ring

- 2 albums of newspaper clippings and certificates about me and other members of my family

- Dad's KKK robes and hoods

- 2 boxes of 12-gauge shotgun ammo that were in the gun

cabinet on Christmas Eve

- a copy of the report – the filed and accepted version by the sheriff's department on Christmas Day 1982.

Once I collected most of what I wanted to, I needed a place to store it. Somewhere safe. Somewhere it wouldn't be easily found. So that weekend, I drove my truck up to one of my uncle's cabins north of town. Picking the lock, I let myself in. I pulled the cord that was hanging down from the ceiling and lowered the stairs leading up to the attic. I stashed everything I had brought with me there, back behind some insulation for safe keeping.

I never told a soul. It was the ace in my pocket should I ever need it.

THE ESCALATION

27
RAMPING UP

As happens with all tragedies, time moves on and everyone else's lives get back to normal. The worst part about life for me was that my mom was gone. I missed her so much! Add to that, no one else really knew the truth of what happened.

Unrecognized grief is extraordinarily painful. It's one thing when people know your story and what you are mourning. It's a completely different thing when they don't have a clue as to why the loss and anger is eating you up inside.

If my own battles against depression and fear weren't enough, my new normal found me desperately fighting to hold onto my reputation as a smart and dependable teenager. Over the next few months and years, my dad would make certain that no one trusted me any further than they could throw me. I think it was his way of making sure that if I ever did speak up about what he did, my credibility would be in doubt.

Dad definitely saw me as a threat to his kingdom. I don't know if he believed I could actually prove that he shot mom, but he definitely knew if I ever mentioned it to anyone, the heat would be turned up much higher than he could possibly control.

His abuse of me was not new. But now his anger toward me was elevated. It had become more than just annoyance and irritation. It was fueled out of desperation and his desire to protect a lifestyle, one that retained the admiration from people that he so desperately enjoyed.

28

Deer Hunt

A couple of weeks into January, a good family friend invited me and my friends to come out to their farm early one Saturday. It was time for one of his wife's Famous Lynda Lochner's Breakfast and the family deer hunt. I don't think they put too much thought into the fact that I wouldn't want to be near any guns. But Dad insisted that I go.

It was in the pre-dawn hours that day. I was already awake as I wasn't sleeping much those days and was dressed and ready. Will and his father were stopping by the house to pick me up. I saw the headlights reflect off of my bedroom wall, and gathered my stuff to head out the door. Just before I reached for the door handle on their truck, my dad ran up behind me.

"You forgot this," he announced, holding out a gun to me.

Would you believe he had the nerve and the audacity to send me to the hunt with a 12 gauge? Yes, you guessed it. The very 12-gauge used that night. The only 12-gauge we owned. It had been only three weeks since the incident. How did Dad manage to get the gun back from the sheriff's office already?

Disgusted, I snatched it out of his hand and climbed into the cab of Will's truck.

Once we finished a huge breakfast – scrambled eggs, bacon, toast and jelly, grits, biscuits and gravy – we headed out to hunt. We were spaced out in the edge of the trees along a pipeline road. The idea was that the dogs would chase the deer out into the clearing. I didn't realize until I was in the woods waiting, that I had no ammo for the gun with me. None. Not a single shotgun shell. I had left all them in the truck.

I obviously wasn't going to get a deer unless I smacked one of them on the head with an empty gun, so I settled into my space and began to think. I held the gun up to my chin with one arm supporting the butt of the shotgun, just like the sheriff's report said my mom had done. More accurately, I *tried* to hold it up. I was a strong 16-year-old young man, and I couldn't hold it there. So how had she been able to do it? I was stronger than her, with longer arms. I wasn't able to reach the trigger! How could law enforcement actually believe that is what had happened?

29

Under His Thumb

There were many times that my friends and I would be swimming in the pool, or playing football or basketball outside. Dad would come out, yell at me for something, and send everyone home. He would punish me because we tore up the grass or trampled a bush or messed up the goal. Basically, we were having too much fun.

He would verbally degrade me any chance he got. Sometimes it was just in front of my sister and brother. More often, it happened in front of my friends. He would call me names. He would make fun of my looks, or my grades, or my abilities, constantly trying to embarrass me and humiliate me. He would lie and accuse me of wrongdoing I literally had nothing to do with. He tried to discredit me by planting money in large amounts in my room, then calling the Sheriff's Department to come find it and arrest me or put me on probation. He also had me committed to a local psych hospital. Twice.

Anything to make me look bad, my dad made it his mission do it.

At the same time, he would do nice things for me. He would buy me new stereo equipment and sporting gear and such. He would allow me to get pretty much anything I asked for. It was this yo-yo existence that drove me crazy. I never knew what to expect out of him. The mind games were endless.

Through the next few months I was often picked up by different sheriff deputies for various crimes and activities. I would get hauled in, dumped into the Sheriff's office, and then my dad would show up to take me home. No charges were ever filed. Nothing was made official. But the rumors and appearances were enough to tarnish my integrity.

The one time I pushed back against what they were accusing me of? My dad left me to spend a night in jail. Message received. So I continued playing the game, knowing that I would be better off not resisting. At least I got to sleep in my own bed that way.

I will completely own up to the mistakes and wrongdoings that I have committed throughout my life. And there are plenty of those. But those during that time were all pickups initiated by my dad – even the ones for speeding!

My dad was powerful among his friends. He basically controlled the region on many fronts. These "good ol' boys" all exchanged favors to keep their standard of living how they liked it. They controlled the narrative of things that happened in that jurisdiction. My dad simply wanted to discredit me and any claims I might make. And through these guys, he had the resources to do it.

30

DITCH

I found myself constantly exhausted from the head games and abuse by dad. I was struggling to sleep at night. I was feeling lonely. I missed my mom. And I couldn't see a way out from underneath my dad's tyranny. I had lost the little hope I had managed to hold on to up to that point.

One night my youth choir was singing at a prison facility north of town. At the time I was living closer to the facility than I was to my church, so I decided to drive myself rather than ride the bus with my friends.

About halfway there, I found myself thinking, "I should just end things now." The pain of death seemed shallow compared to what I was feeling. I passed a couple of places that looked like a good place to drive off of a bridge into a creek in order to end things. The next bridge I approached, I shut my eyes, gripped the steering wheel, and yanked to the right. I heard the crash, felt my truck lurch downward, then quiet. I shook my head and rubbed my eyes. Damn.

Instead of flipping and landing upside down, my truck simply bounced off of the guardrail, spun around and landed in a shallow ditch. I checked my limbs. Fine. I looked for blood. None. Amazingly, I was completely unhurt.

Less than 5 minutes later, the bus carrying everyone else came along. The driver slowed to a stop when the bus headlights illuminated a truck off the road in the ditch. The music director hopped off and walked slowly over to the truck. To his surprise, he recognized the occupant. Me.

"Evan!" He tapped on my window and I lowered it so we could talk.

"Hey," I responded.

"You okay?" he asked.

"Yeah, I said," Not wanting to admit my original intention. "I must have lost control. These roads are super slippery right now."

He helped me out of my truck and up the hill to the bus door. A few seconds later, I was riding the rest of the way with my friends, and no one had a clue that I had just attempted to end my life.

31
carrying

I survived my first suicide attempt without a scratch and without anyone knowing what I had even tried to do. But with the mental abuse, head games, and threats from my dad continuing to increase, I decided I needed some kind of protection.

I started carrying a small .25 Browning automatic with me everywhere I went. It came in handy just a few days later. I carried that thing everywhere. School, church, choir, store, bed. I was nearly never without it on me, or at least within arm's length.

My dad came at me with his fist one time. He landed a couple of blows, and then reached behind him for a skillet sitting on one of the burners on the kitchen stove. As soon as he grabbed the handle, I pulled the gun out of the back of my waistband.

I pointed it right at him.

He froze.

"Don't!" I ordered. "Don't. Move."

I brought my other hand up to steady the gun. Here was my opportunity to put an end to all of the abuse. This was my chance to put an end to my dad. I ran through all the scenarios in my mind. It was probably only a couple of seconds, but it felt like an eternity.

I could literally end this monster's life right here, right now. I could be free from all of his bullying and anger.

But I couldn't do it. I wasn't a killer. Even if he deserved it, I just couldn't freakin' do it. I couldn't pull the trigger and end him.

So I took a deep breath. Me, with the gun aimed at his chest, and him, holding a skillet about waist height.

"If you ever come near me again, I *will* kill you."

We both knew I was dead serious.

I backed away slowly, dropped the gun to my side and retreated into my room.

It didn't end Dad's abuse and head games against me, but it did let him know I would fight back. I was no longer afraid of him.

But the truth of the matter was that deep inside, I still was afraid.

Dad tried to confiscate the gun every chance he got, mostly when he suspected it might not be on me. But he could never find it no matter how much he searched. Little did he know I also had retrieved a small sub-nose .38 special revolver that he had once used as a probation and parole officer. I found that one, too, as I needed a backup in case he eventually found the other gun.

I practiced shooting anytime I could find the time and place, which was fairly often. I was deadly accurate with both guns. I even contemplated shooting myself in the leg or something with his .38 and trying to frame him. But that would never have worked. Not me against my dad and all of his cronies.

I was stuck. The best I could do was to try and protect myself.

32

Remodel

About that time, Dad decided that it was time for him to remodel the house.

He walked into my bedroom one day and sat down on the edge of my bed. "Evan, let's talk."

The hair on my neck stood up. I wasn't sure where this conversation was going, but I slowly responded, "Okay... Why?"

Dad quickly put on his jolly, easy-going personality and took a seat in my desk chair. Leaning back, he crossed his legs. "I'm planning on doing some work around the house," he stated, "change things up a bit. My plan is to take this room — your bedroom — add a bathroom to it, and combine it with part of the garage to make a new master bedroom suite."

I stared through him. "Yeah?"

"And then take my bedroom, renovate it, and make it yours."

"What the hell?" I thought to myself.

When I raised my eyebrows, he added, "You'll have your very own bathroom. And we will add an exterior door to it for you to come and go at will. You know, give you more independence around here." And then followed up, "anything else you want to add to it?"

"No." I shook my head and bit my bottom lip.

He slapped his thighs with both palms and stood up, as if to say "that's that, then," and left my room.

It would be a cold day in hell before I would even re-enter the room where I witnessed my mom's cold, lifeless body and smelled the stench of her blood and death. I had avoided even going back to that part of the house since Christmas morning.

And my dad actually wanted me to live in that space? He was a far crazier bastard than I thought! Or maybe he simply knew I would refuse to go along with it, and it was an easy way for him to get me out of his house.

Maybe his goal of encouraging my exit worked. Because I sure as hell wasn't having any of that plan of his.

33

Garage

The following weekend, I moved most of my belongings up the hill behind the house to a 2-car garage that my dad had built. I would just sleep and live up there. I had to get out from underneath the roof of the "hell house" as I called it.

Although Derek and Julia asked why I was moving out, Dad never questioned it. I believe he knew. And, he obviously didn't care.

One day my buddy Brent and I were hanging out up there, shooting the shit and just being boys.

We had been fishing at the pond close by and hadn't had much luck. So we had returned to the garage and started up a game of 2 Card Poker. I was winning pretty handily when my dad walked up.

He was holding a .410 shotgun down by his side.

"Evan, did you track mud through the kitchen this afternoon?"

"Uh, no. I haven't even been in the house today," I replied.

"You lying little s.o.b!" Dad blasted back.

I pled my case again, replaying what we had done and where we had been earlier. I could see the red begin flooding his face. Before either Brent or me knew what was happening, he shouldered the rifle and pulled the trigger. It hit the garage door about a foot above my head from where I had been sitting, leaving a huge hole.

Brent was petrified. He couldn't move. He just sat there wide-eyed while my dad continued his rant. I couldn't believe he was this upset over a little dirt in the house. Although Dad rarely needed a reason to unload on me.

"You better tell me the truth, boy!" he yelled.

I stood up – so quickly that I became a bit dizzy. "I AM telling the truth!"

I ran toward my dad and buried my shoulder into his stomach, knocking him off of his feet. We fought on the ground for a minute or two, with each of us trading having the upper hand. Before I knew it, everything went dark.

Dad had grabbed a baseball bat and hit me in the head with it, cracking my skull open. I put my hand up to my head. There was blood everywhere. This time my dad had a problem.

A witness.

I think he then realized he had two options:

(1) let me bleed out and have another murder on his hands, or

(2) get me to the hospital and make up yet another story about how my injury occurred.

Brent had come over on the ground and knelt beside me, trying anything to stop the bleeding. My dad grabbed Brent by the elbow and stood him up. He leaned into Brent's ear and growled. I couldn't hear what he said, but he must have threatened him strongly, because Brent lost whatever color in his face that he had managed to maintain up to that point.

They both carried me down the hill, over to the station wagon, and put me in the back. After eighteen stitches and two days in the hospital, I was released to go home. To this day, I have a huge knot and a 6-inch scar from that incident.

By this point, I knew I not only wanted to get out of town. I knew that I absolutely *must* escape... before my dad actually killed me.

THE ESCAPE AND RETURN

34

ENLISTED

I came up with a plan to join the army. I couldn't stand to be around the house and my dad, and I was even getting tired of hearing everyone say they were "sorry for my loss" and "what could they do" and "you poor thing." It seemed I was always short of breath and my chest felt heavy anytime I was around other people.

Enlisting made sense to me. I would be out and away from my dad's influence, thus insuring my safety and hopefully my sanity. I would make new friends who didn't know anything about my life and its problems. I would learn skills that I could use for my future. I would make my own money. And it would give me reason to exist beyond serving as a punching bag for my dad.

The issue was that I had to wait a few months until I was old enough, in order to officially report. So I used that time to get my GED and to take college level entry placement exams.

The husband of one of my dad's secretaries was the GED teacher. I never even had to take the test. Dad made sure I encountered no obstacles, hurdles, or speed bumps on my way to joining in the military. In hindsight maybe he was hoping I would get killed or something. Regardless, he definitely wanted me out of the area and did everything he could to help expedite the process.

Finally and not nearly soon enough — on my birthday — I left for basic training. I didn't tell anyone I was going. I didn't say any goodbyes. I simply woke up, drove to North Carolina, and reported for duty.

I had been in the service for almost a year when I re-injured my leg from an old football injury. Well, honestly it was the same knee my dad had bashed with the firewood, but I didn't tell my superiors that. I simply asked them what my options were, given the situation.

The Army told me I would need to find something different to do now, since my busted knee would no longer allow me jump out of airplanes. They gave me the choice to either change my MOS (Method of Service) or to be medically discharged from the 82nd airborne infantry. My knowledge of the options available to me was limited, and I was incredibly disappointed to no longer be training in jump school. I honestly didn't know what else I wanted to do. So I chose the discharge.

I was returning home.

I was well aware of what adversarial challenges awaited me there, but I felt stronger from my time in basic training and the experience I had gained during my year away. I was just about to turn 18. I thought I could now handle my dad and whatever he did to me. Little did I know how wrong I was.

35

Legal Woes

Once I arrived home, I moved back into the garage. The bullet hole was still there.

As if I needed a reminder.

It didn't take me too long before I found myself in trouble, this time mostly of my own doing. I had begun dating a girl who was sixteen, almost seventeen. Everyone knew she was my girlfriend. She wore my letter jacket and my senior ring. We were together as much as we were allowed to be.

However, when my 18th birthday arrived, and she was still under the legal age of consent, I was arrested for unlawful carnal knowledge. I've always figured it was another dad-setup, since no one else seemed to complain or even notice, including her parents. But regardless, simply given our ages I knew there was no way to contest the charge, especially in a stacked case such as mine.

I ended up pleading guilty to contributing to the delinquency of a juvenile. That was only a misdemeanor so it wouldn't drag me down with a record. But it did cost me six months of time at the penal farm.

Not long after finishing up my sentence, I was hanging out in what was looking more and more like a furnished garage apartment now.

I had been eyeing a 1972 roadrunner that I had seen on a local used car lot. Not only eyeing, but also trying to get Dad to buy it for me. He actually drove me to the dealer on a Sunday. They were closed. (Back in those days, Blue Laws were very common. They were legislative measures that restricted or banned some or all activities and shopping on specified days — most often on Sundays in the United States).

Even though the dealership was closed, it was parked outside by the service entrance door. Dad told me that he had made previous arrangements for me to get the car. "It's ready, the keys are in it. Go ahead and drive it off." Then he added, "We will finish up the paperwork on it tomorrow."

You would have thought by now that I knew better than to trust him. But I really wanted the car, so I decided to go with it.

About 15 minutes down the road, I looked in the rearview mirror to see flashing lights. I glanced down at the speedometer. I wasn't speeding, so what the heck was I getting pulled over for?

The officer approached me, "License and registration, please."

I gave him my license and then began to explain.

"Sir, this car has been reported stolen," he informed me.

"What the hell...? Wait. My dad just took me to pick this car up," I replied. "He said that he bought it for..." My voice trailed off and I hung my head.

I was arrested and taken to the local jail. I did a little time at that facility for possessing stolen property, and then was sent back to my town to face the actual auto theft charge.

36

College

I soon appeared before a judge on the auto theft charge. After handing down my sentence, the judge told me that he would suspend that sentence and only issue me probation, under one condition. The condition was that I would immediately enroll at a university or some type of school and attend until I finished my degree.

I had taken a whole bunch of college level entry placement tests the year before when I was waiting to leave for basic training. My scores on them were very high, earning me enough credits to practically begin college as a sophomore. Of course I would take him up on that offer. I was released from jail and began school the next week.

The campus where I registered to attend was about an hour from home. I thought that distance would give me enough of a buffer to be protected from my dad. But once again, I was wrong. We quickly fell right back into the same yo-yo song and dance.

Dad paid for tuition and for my room and board.

He paid for a car for me — a legitimate purchase this time.

He also paid for my illegal drugs. Yes, you read that right. He supported my drug habit by making them easily accessible. I probably had some of the best drugs to come into our part of the state during that time. It made perfect sense in his warped way of thinking. If I was using drugs, he maintained his control over me. His hope was probably that I would become addicted, which I eventually did. But he would always have the fallback of having me arrested for possession if I didn't.

Dad was using my trust fund to pay for tuition and everything else. Somewhere down the road after I completed my first year in college, we had a huge falling out. So in order to remind me who really held all the cards, he stopped paying my tuition from my trust fund.

The school notified me that they were dropping my enrollment shortly after that. I packed up everything from the dorm and headed home. Before I even got back to the house, my dad had already called the sheriff's department. They were waiting for me in the driveway to arrest me for breaking the condition of my suspended sentence. I never even got to unpack.

They took me into custody and hauled me back to the now-all-too-familiar jail cell.

37

Leaving

Sitting on that cold steel bench inside the walls of my cell, I faced the realization that my options were running out. I was broke, depressed, lonely and quickly becoming hopeless.

My attorney informed me that the court would allow me to leave the state if I promised to stay away. I was a bit confused by the logic of that; but if it would get me out of the God-forsaken place I was experiencing, I was all for it. I was never told how long I had to stay out-of-state. But they made it clear that if I ever came back, they would arrest me on the old warrants.

A week later, I was released from jail and taken straight to the airport. My godmother, Miss Janessa, and her husband had agreed to take me in. They were up in Fairbanks, Alaska. Her husband was in the Air Force and stationed there.

Miss Janessa was especially important to me. She had played a maternal role in my life since I had been a very young child. My dad initially hired her to help around the house, but she soon became family. She was a housekeeper, nanny, and confidant. More importantly, she was my friend.

There was one day that my brother and sister and I were playing. Miss Janessa was folding laundry. Julia had found these white sheet things in my dad's closet and she and Derek were running through the house pretending to be ghosts and I was giving chase. None of us knew the gravity of what we were doing – as we had no idea that they had stumbled upon were KKK robes.

As we ran past the coffee table, Miss Janessa grabbed me by the arm stopping me in my tracks.

"Where did you get those robes?" she loudly whispered through clenched teeth.

I saw the pain and fear and anger in her eyes. "I think Julia found them in a box somewhere in Dad's closet," I revealed.

"Get them from the kids and bring them to me. Right now!"

I told Julia and Derek we could no longer play with the robes and they begrudgingly let me take them. I brought them back to Miss Janessa. Tears were flowing down her dark-skinned face. I don't know what she did with them, but I never saw them again until I searched and found them when I was gathering up incriminating stuff to take to the cabin after mom's death.

None of us knew the significance of what had happened that day with Miss Janessa until we were older. We had no idea what the robes were for or what they represented. And we certainly didn't share my dad's hatred.

The fact that Miss Janessa was willing to take me into her home in Alaska spoke volumes of the kind of person she was. Kind, pure-hearted, loving, and generous.

When I landed in Alaska, and walked out of the airport, the biting winds hurt my face. The temperature was over 60 degrees colder than where I left. I was in for a rude awakening.

38

vegas

A couple of years later, Miss Janessa and James had to move due to his changing Air Force assignment. I stayed in Alaska for about five more years. Dad was constantly sending me drug money. Well, actually what I called it was "hush money." He would do pretty much anything that would help keep me out of his state and keep quiet about what I knew.

I was a messed up young adult. The trauma and secrecy of what I had experienced kept pulling me under. I couldn't sleep. Nightmares about that Christmas Eve night seemed to haunt me every time I closed my eyes. I found certain drugs that would help me stay awake (with my rationale that I wouldn't have nightmares if I didn't sleep). My job didn't provide enough money to support my new-found addiction, so I began stealing and dealing on the side. As shrewd as I tried to be, some of my misdeeds would eventually catch up with me, so I would spend time on and off in jail.

I had purposefully cut ties to any and everything to do with my family and my hometown. I was convinced they didn't want me. And consequently, I convinced myself I didn't need them. A lot of the best relationships can often be difficult. But relationships not based in honesty are useless. And I couldn't be honest about the one thing that defined my existence.

Armchair psychologists and counselors might think I should have just gotten over it. Or not have allowed myself to be defined by one night. Easier said than done. Believe me, I've tried.

I eventually moved to Las Vegas, hoping a change of scenery would help to calm my nightmares and set me on the straight and narrow. A new start. A new chapter. A new life.

But my move soon proved to be only just that — a change of scenery. I found myself caught back up in the same routine. I had gotten to be a bit smarter as a criminal though. The illegal activities I chose in Vegas proved to be more lucrative and less dangerous. However they came with a higher price tag when I got caught: longer sentences in tougher prisons.

Honestly, the jail time for my various offenses through those years is one of those things that probably saved my life. Being incarcerated forced me to detox. And as bad as the food was, at least I ate consistent meals. Continuous drug usage would have put me six feet under in due time.

39

Unbearable Life

Not that six feet under wasn't appealing to me at times.

Numerous times throughout the years, I would find myself with cold sweats, pistol loaded, hammer cocked, and a gun to my head or in my mouth. I begged and pleaded with God.

"Where are you?"

"Why is my life so f*cked up?"

"Why did my dad have to be such a monster?"

"Why couldn't mom have lived?"

"Why do I keep doing stupid shit?"

"When will this whirlwind of my life calm down?"

Each time I found myself like this, I stayed alive. Too chicken to pull the trigger, I guess.

Except for one time.

The muzzle of the gun was pressed into my temple. I squeezed the trigger. It misfired. Nothing but a click.

I re-cocked it, checked it, and pointed it at a family photo on my dresser, specifically at my dad. Squeezed the trigger again. The gun fired.

Same bullet, same pistol. Misfired on me, but fired at the picture.

What was God telling me to do? Was he trying to keep me from killing myself?

I prayed for answers and got none. I begged for help and none came. The nightmares continued. Drugs no longer helped. Then the daymares started. I would hallucinate while wide awake.

I overdosed multiple times on purpose. I didn't care if I died or not, I simply wanted the pain to end. But somehow — like it or not — I always survived.

40

Train Tracks

I served a fairly long sentence while in Vegas. A lot of jail time, a lot of alone time, a lot of quiet time.

The hurt and pain and deep thoughts and prayers and dreams helped me to figure out and unravel the mess of my life that Dad and I had caused. I had a ton of emotions all rolled into one.

I eventually came to my senses. I realized that the way I had been living life was absolutely no way to exist. Regardless of what I had experienced, it was time to clean up my act and leave the drugs and crimes behind. I am proud to say I have done just that. Clean and honest living for almost a decade now.

My life didn't suddenly start to begin coming up roses after my epiphany. I was consciously choosing to not depend on chemicals to help me face my demons. And I was not committing crimes anymore. My life continued to remain extremely difficult. And I was sober — which meant feeling everything once again.

During my initial time out of state, when my brother and sister were still kids into young adulthood, I would mail home birthday cards and Christmas cards for them. I found out years later that they had never received them. Figure that one out. I don't know if Dad burned them or simply stashed them away. But Julia and Derek never had a way to know I was thinking about them or celebrating their milestones.

Hence, my brother and sister grew up thinking I didn't care about them anymore. A fair assessment on their part, considering we had no contact. The only person that ever knew where I was, other than my dad, was Miss Janessa. And that was only because she was the one I called whenever I truly needed something.

Since Miss Janessa and dad were the only two people who ever had any contact with me, no one else ever knew where I was living and what I might be doing. If nobody could find me, nobody could reach out to me. It was by my own design. I had turned my back on all of my friends. And my family — both immediate and extended — never heard from me. The result was that I ended up being lost and forgotten.

So even though I moved back to my home state 30 years after I left, I found myself completely alone. I felt like a loser and a nobody. Homeless and jobless, I was beginning my new lease on life from ground zero. I spent the maximum number of days allowed at the Salvation Army shelter, then slept outside until I found a place I could afford. It was only a room with a mini-fridge that shared a community kitchen and tv room, but it was a roof over my head.

***

On one of my darkest nights, I went for a walk. Approaching the train tracks, I crawled up to the trestle and lay down across the ties. I knew the schedule, and anticipated the nightly train would be there in about 15 minutes. I had timed it perfectly – early enough if the train came early, but not so early that I would lose my nerve.

The stars were out and I could make out the Big Dipper and Orion. I wondered if my mom was up there somewhere looking down on me. After all that had happened, I decided it was time for my life to come to an end. There was no reason for me to stay on Earth any longer.

I grabbed my phone to check the time. Seven more minutes. I exhaled a tired long breath.

An alert pinged on my phone. Looking to see what it was, I discovered someone had sent me a friend request. It was a person who I had grown up with in church. After all of my years of distancing myself from everyone, this person was suddenly now reaching out to me.

I sat up between the railroad ties. I can't say that I didn't still want to die, but my curiosity was piqued enough to make me decide to climb down off of the tracks. After all, the train would come by again tomorrow.

REFLECTIONS

41

Dad

Dad

Dad died a few years back. He had a stroke and other health problems that caused deterioration not only of his physical being, but also his ability to influence folks around town. Consequences of some of his past actions were catching up to him, as he was indicted for some financial crimes. I followed the investigation and such through the newspaper,

I went to visit him in the hospital just after his stroke had left him in a coma. The nurses in ICU told me he could hear and give slight responses, but that I should talk softly to him.

I walked over to his bed, held his hand and whispered in his ear. "Do you know who this is?"

He gave my hand a light squeeze.

"You know," I spoke a bit louder. "I really hope you make it out of your coma, because I have something I want to tell you before you die. And I want to be able to look you in the eye when I say it."

He did regain consciousness from that episode and lived for quite a few more years. When I received word that the end was near, I returned home. He had moved away from the "hell house" into a different home after remarrying. I walked into his house and found him lying in a hospital bed that hospice had set up for him. He was awake, so I leaned down, nose to nose, where only he could hear me.

"I know exactly what you did to mom. I saw it! I hate you and everything you stand for. I hate how you tried to destroy me. I hope you rot in hell, you evil bastard."

He never blinked or flinched. He knew I was speaking the truth.

Two days later, he died.

***

Derek and Julia wanted me to say something at the funeral, probably because I was the oldest sibling. Also probably because neither of them were much into public speaking. Back in my previous life, I had won awards for speaking. But I had no desire to attend, much let participate in our dad's funeral service.

I guess I shouldn't have been surprised they wanted me to do that. I had protected them from the ugly truth for decades. While they knew dad and I didn't get along, they had no idea how deep my hatred of him ran, or why. They had no idea that he had actually killed our mother.

Keeping up the now-decades long charade, I tried to come up with something to say that would be appropriate to share about our dad without blatantly lying. I toyed with the idea of dropping the truth, a bombshell that would still be reverberating today. Seriously. I actually contemplated doing that. But in the end I decided against that strategy. There would be too many people present that were loyal to my dad. And proclaiming the truth publicly and spontaneously would be completely unfair to Julia and Derek. I had spent my whole life shielding them from dad and his evil ways. I wasn't about to start unloading on them now.

So I was back to deciding what to say. Sadly, I could not come up with any happy thoughts of him and our family as a whole. I had none. Nada. Zero. Happy memories of my mom and brother and sister? Yes. But none that included my dad.

So I dug deep down and found the memory of him serving as a timer at Julia and Derek's swim meets, spinning a stopwatch lanyard around his index finger, and cheering them on poolside. That was it. That was the best contribution I had to offer for his memorial service.

***

As you would probably expect if you've read this far, I inherited not one red cent from my father's estate. I'm not sure that I would have even wanted anything from him, but it would have been nice to have a chance to reject it, to have some say in the matter.

Dad had spent every bit of my trust on my tuition, drugs, and cars. So that had a zero balance. As for the assets he possessed, I don't know if Julia and Derek ever received anything or not. I'm sure most of his stuff stayed with his current wife due to community property laws and everything.

Ironically though, Dad managed to find a way to take care of his friends and bedfellows. He owned quite a bit of property in the region, some of which had oil or gas wells on them which only increased their value. Most of the property he owned then is now in their names.

Even after death, he managed to remain true to the good ol' boys.

42

Friendships

These days my friendships are, should I say, still extremely limited in number. I work, I worry, I pay bills, and I talk to my dog. I don't have money to go out, and I'm not sure I would do that even if I could afford it (although the occasional nicely-seared steak would be nice). Sleep is still hard to come by, especially during the holiday season and around important dates. I don't rest well and the nightmares still haven't stopped.

I had a super strong friend group in middle school and early high school. There were about 8-10 of us guys who were inseparable. We had nicknames for everyone, and even had a name for our group. We were always hanging out and having fun together. Rarely would you see one of us without at least 1 or 2 others there tagging along. Sometimes we caused a bit of mischief, but nothing ever too bad.

We mostly played Nerf football, wrestled, goofed off, started water balloon fights, TP'd yards of friends and teachers, and had basketball dunking contests. There is no telling how many rims we bent and backboards we broke from jumping off mini-trampolines and attempting crazy NBA All-Star style dunks!

The more time that passed after my mom's death, the more I became separated and distanced from the group. It wasn't their fault. Quite the opposite, in fact. They all tried to keep me involved. But I began to withdraw into my own dreadful little world and isolate. I simply couldn't allow them to get too close to the secrets and darkness of what had happened. It was necessary for me to keep them out, simply in order to survive.

I wholeheartedly regret that now.

I miss the days of laughter and mischief-making. I long for the times filled with high-fives and nick-names. I need those places now where I can be myself and still be embraced as one of the group. I deeply long for a place to belong.

Perhaps if I reached out to them, they might take me back? I wouldn't blame them for wanting nothing to do with me, though. I abandoned them, not the other way around.

43

Family Matters

After my mom's death, her parents were obviously at the funeral; but after that day, I saw them only two other times. I separated myself from them and from my aunts and uncles on both sides of the family. I wanted no questions and no reminders.

They were obviously made aware of the "trouble" that I was getting myself into. Little did they know all my "problems" were mostly orchestrated by dear old Dad. My guess is that they just figured that after losing my mom, I had gone off the deep end. Or, maybe they thought getting into trouble was my way of begging for attention and just acting out.

But I had purposefully created distance to keep them out of harm's way, and to keep my screwed up family matters private. If I'm being completely honest, it was for their protection *and* mine. To this day, I've had no contact with any of my relatives, with the exception of Julia and Derek in recent years. Even then it's only occasionally with her and more rarely with him.

Keeping the secret of my mom's murder and shouldering Dad's abuse was necessary to protect my sister and brother. I bore the brunt of Dad's anger and hate to keep it off of and away from them. Even though that came at a high cost to my own well-being, I wasn't going to allow him to ruin their lives, too.

There were four men who came into my life shortly before my mom died and remained for years after. I will always believe they were angels, or messengers of God. They had a sense that something wasn't right in my life. They saw beyond the surface. I had been a straight A student, debate team leader, healthy athlete, and church goer. But I suddenly became subdued and prone to trouble. I can only imagine that they saw and heard my cries for help, saw something that caused them to reach out to me.

A fireman, a musician, a minister, and a friend's dad. These were each men of great faith. Not merely church-going folks, but men who lived out their belief in a God who loved us all. Even though I was raised in church and could quote more scripture verses than most anyone, I couldn't understand a God who would allow what I had experienced. The abuse and events that happened in my own life didn't make sense to me.

Nonetheless, their advice and concern and example didn't go to waste. Their attempts to reach me planted seeds of love and hope. That is what has helped keep me alive and somewhat sane through those long dark years and even in these recent days. These men were my chosen heroes, my true father figures. Only one of the four is still alive today, but I pray someway, somehow, they are able to know the magnitude of their influence in my life. Family members or not, they helped me to survive. They helped me get to *this* place. The place of finally telling and living the truth.

EPILOGUE

I drive along the 2-lane road that leads north of town. The hood of my truck is covered in yellow, and the spring wind is blowing the pollen around. My window is rolled all the way down and 70's rock is playing loudly from my playlist. As I pass through the farmlands and cattle, a familiar aroma hits me. It is the smell of happier days.

Happier days that existed before my dad started hitting me. Happier days before I found out that the monster who adopted me was actually my biological dad. Happier days before he killed my mom. And happier days when the love of friends and family was abundant.

My heart begins to beat faster and faster as I approach the turnoff to the cabin. I'm not sure who even lives there now, or if anyone even does. I don't know if it's still in the family or not. Hell, I'm just hoping the structure is still standing. Cause I'm banking my money on the fact that all the stuff that I stashed back in 1983 will still be there.

I'm not sure how you ask someone if you can come in their house and look for something you hid in their attic forty years ago, but that's exactly what I'm about to do. I'm going to walk up and knock on the door. I'll introduce myself, and then I'll ask for permission to look for my possessions.

I don't really need them for me. I was there. I know what happened. But there are items that will reveal the truth to others of what happened that horrendous night. They will also redefine who people knew my father to be. And it's time to bring them into the light.

It's time to start crushing secrets.

Afterword
A Note from the Author

The story you have just read is based on true happenings. Names and defining details and dialogues have been changed or invented, so this is technically a work of fiction. However, much of what you have just finished reading actually happened.

With the recent invention of podcasts, and true crime[1] genre's rise in popularity, our awareness of cover-ups and manipulation of our justice system has spiked. Alex Murdaugh, Grant Solomon, the Long Island Serial Killer, and Ellen Rae Greenberg are just a handful of cases illustrate the influence that powerful individuals wield and the corruption that exists among law enforcement.

Only the most naive of us believe that justice always unfolds. Corruption, manipulation of the system, and cover-ups are as old as time. And although the vast majority of people in our judicial and law enforcement systems are honorable, any one of them who abuses the power entrusted to them, is one too many.

---

1. True crime is a nonfiction literary, podcast, and film genre in which the author examines a crime and details the actions of people associated with and affected by criminal events.

Growing up alongside Evan, I was well-acquainted with his family and friends. I vividly remember hearing about his mom's death and feeling its impact.

Her suicidal death was always somewhat suspicious to me. I worked with her in our church music department on a weekly basis and never knew her to be anything but kind, compassionate, and joyful. In my young teenage mind, her suicide just didn't compute.

Over the years, I found out that others shared in my suspicions — my own father included. A close friend and law enforcement officer said that he almost assuredly knew that she didn't kill herself; but he was unable to prove it at that point. He carried that burden to his grave.

As I began working on this book, I discovered more and more people who never bought the narrative of her death. A historian in our hometown revealed his doubts to me through text messages. Probably the biggest eye-opener to me came when a close friend recently referred to this tragedy as being as the town's "worst kept secret."

While Evan may find a bit of comfort in knowing his secret wasn't so secret, I am heart-broken.

We all failed him.

Miserably.

Evan's dad was the bully of the century. Yet none of us risked standing up to him. We all remained bystanders. And even worse, some of us were enablers.

What might have been — had we given voice to our suspicions? What might life look like now? It's impossible to know. But to try to rewrite the past or impart justice now, would merely be an act of futility.

But we can start today and move forward changing the narrative. We can speak up for those who are victimized. We can reach out to those who are lonely. We can offer fresh starts to those who have been abused. We can call out injustice and manipulation. We can fight for those who have no voice.

Together we *can* make a difference.

Resources

Life is often difficult for all of us.
Please reach out if you are experiencing any of these mental health challenges:

Suicide

https://988lifeline.org

Domestic Violence

1-800-799-SAFE (7233)
https://www.thehotline.org
Text START to 88788

Substance Abuse

https://www.aa.org
https://www.na.org
National 1-800-662-HELP (4357)

Anxiety and Depression

https://adaa.org

Homelessness Shelter Resources
https://nche.ed.gov/shelter/

Made in the USA
Coppell, TX
17 June 2024